This book belongs to...

For my brother John - P.B.

For Kate - C.C.

First published in Great Britain in 2016
by Fourth Wall Publishing
2 Riverview Business Park,
Shore Wood Road, Bromborough,
Wirral, Merseyside CH62 3RQ

ISBN:978-1-91-085130-2

Printed in Turkey.

**fourth wall
publishing**

WRITTEN BY
PAUL BROWN

ILLUSTRATED BY
CHRIS CAPSTICK

Building sandcastles was one of Marcel's
favourite pastimes.

He would spend hours on the beach with his
dog Whippy, creating amazing sculptures
out of sand, shells and pebbles.

But annoyingly, when the tide
came in, Marcel's lovely creations
were always washed away.

He tried building his sandcastles
further away from the sea,
but the sand was just too dry and
wouldn't stick together.

He dug really deep moats around
them, but they eventually
filled up with seawater
and his creations crumbled.

No matter how big and strong Marcel built his
sandcastles, the sea was always bigger and stronger!

"EUREKA!"

Before bedtime, as Marcel was washing the sand
out from his toes, he had an amazing idea!

"THAT'S IT!" he exclaimed. The sea was just like
a gigantic bath – he would simply unplug it!

Without delay, Marcel got
straight to work!
"Whippy, we're going to need something
special to get to the bottom of the sea!"

With nuts and bolts
and springs and screws,
Whippy and Marcel worked
late into the night...

...until finally, with the last
whizz of his drill, the diving
machine was ready!

Full of excitement, Marcel raced to the beach to launch it.
Luckily, it was high tide, so with a splash and a zoom
of his propeller, he disappeared below the surface.

Marcel travelled deeper and deeper underwater,
past all kinds of weird and wonderful sea creatures
until he eventually spotted the plug!

The old chain was extremely heavy and it took all of
Marcel's strength to lift it to the surface.

Back in the boat, Marcel attached
the chain to his crane.

"Hoist her up Whippy!"

Suddenly, there was a loud
gurgling noise, and as the plug
came up, the sea started to
disappear down a huge whirlpool!

Their little boat swirled around as the
ocean drained away, until they eventually found
themselves washed up on the rocks.

All around Marcel, the creatures of the sea
were trapped on the sand and in the shallow
rock pools with no means of escape.

Then Marcel realised that without the sea,
the frozen ice caps would begin to melt and the polar
bears and penguins would have nowhere to live.

He needed to fix things... and fast!

"That's it!" shouted Marcel
as he jumped to his feet.

"If there was a plughole, surely
there must also be a tap!"

But where could it be?

And would they be able to find it in time to
save all the creatures that need the sea?

For hours, Marcel and Whippy trudged
through the soggy sand, searching
for the mysterious sea tap...

Yap!

Yap!

Just as they were about to give up,
Whippy started barking!
"That's it boy, but how do we reach it?"

Then, Whippy gave Marcel an idea.

With miles and miles of sand all around, they started to build...

...the biggest, most fantastic
sandcastle EVER!

At the top, with a huff and a puff, a push and a pull...

...the tap finally turned on!

With the force of a waterfall, the sea blasted out, sending
Marcel and Whippy tumbling down into the rising water below!

Washed onto the beach by huge waves,
Marcel and Whippy were wet and exhausted –
but very relieved!

Quickly, the oceans filled back up.
Dolphins were delighted,
crabs were content and
the octopus was overjoyed!

The sea froze to make ice
and the polar bears and penguins
returned to their homes.

Finally, with everything back to normal,
Marcel didn't mind that his sandcastles got washed away
– because he can build a bigger and better one every day!